For Cynthea Liu, who always means business
—T. S.

For Broccoli Kallock
—J. M.

ISBN 978-0-545-45118-5

Text copyright © 2011 by Tammi Sauer.
Illustrations copyright © 2011 by Jeff Mack.
All rights reserved. Published by Scholastic Inc., 557 Broadway, New York, NY 10012,
by arrangement with Simon & Schuster Books for Young Readers, an imprint of Simon & Schuster Children's
Publishing Division. SCHOLASTIC and associated logos are trademarks and/or registered trademarks of Scholastic Inc.

12 11 10 9 8 7 6 5 4 3 2 1   12 13 14 15 16 17/0

Printed in the U.S.A.   08

First Scholastic printing, January 2012

Book design by Lucy Ruth Cummins
The text for this book is set in Graham.
The illustrations for this book are rendered in acrylic.

Mr. Duck lived by himself at the pond.
Each day he followed a tight schedule.

From 6:00 in the morning until 7:00, he would stretch his wings.

From 7:00 until 8:00, he would fluff his feathers.

At precisely 8:01, he would glide across the perfectly still water.

"Ah," said Mr. Duck. "It's so peaceful. So quiet. I have everything I need."

Day after day, week after week, and year after year, everything was the same.

And Mr. Duck was very happy.

Then one especially hot summer day, Mr. Duck had just begun his morning gliding when he saw . . .

Pig?

But Pig did *not* get the message.

Mr. Duck was all set to give Pig a strongly worded speech regarding private property when . . .

"Well, there you are," said Cow.
"Let's see your moooves," called
Pig. "Jump in!"

"You don't mind, do you, Mr. Duck?"
said Cow as she
plowed past.

"Moo, mooooo."
SPLASH!

Mr. Duck grumbled.

He mumbled.

He flip-flop-fumbled.

But Pig and Cow did *not* get the message.

Mr. Duck was all set to tell them what's what when . . .

"Hey!" said Goat. "We've been looking all over for you!"

"Anyone up for a game of Marco Polo?" called Pig.

"Last one in is a rotten egg!" cheeped a chick.

"C'mon, Mr. Duck!" said Cow. "You're it!"

The water got wild. The scenery got crowded.
And the peace and quiet?

It.
Was.
Gone.

Mr. Duck tapped.

He flapped.

He totally SNAPPED.

"QUA-A-A-A-A-ACKKK!"
And somebody got the message.

"Perhaps we've overstayed our welcome," said Chick.

"*Oh*," said the other animals.

"Out! Out! Out of *my* pond!" cried Mr. Duck.

"This time I mean business!"

"So sorry."

"My apologies."

"Good-bye for GOOD!" said Mr. Duck.

"Sorry to have bothered you," said Chick.
"Thanks for letting us swim in your pond."

Alone at last, Mr. Duck returned to his routine.

He stretched his wings.

There was no splashy belly flopping.

He fluffed his feathers.

There was no annoying water ballet.

He glided across the perfectly still water.

There was certainly no rowdy round of Marco Polo.

"Ah," said Mr. Duck. "It's so peaceful. So quiet. And that's just the way I like it!"

On Monday:
Quiet.

On Tuesday:
Very quiet.

On Wednesday:
Peaceful.

On Thursday:
Very peaceful.

On Friday:
YAWWWWNNN.

On Saturday:
Mr. Duck twiddled his
feathers. Peacefully and
quietly, of course.

And on Sunday?

PROPERTY
OF MR.
DUCK

NO
TRESPASS

Mr. Duck had a plan!

These days Mr. Duck
still loves to stretch at
6:00.

He still loves to fluff his
feathers at 7:00.

He still loves to glide across the perfectly still water at precisely 8:01.

But sometimes life calls for a little noise . . .

especially with friends.